Ho, Ho, Ho...
Easter is on it's Way!

Easter break is around the corner and young Junie can't wait to get a break from school and wake up to a basket full of goodies! It's the next best thing after Christmas, and she begins to wonder if it is more like Christmas than she realized.

Gina Brundage

Ho, Ho, Ho...

Easter is on it's Way!

Xulon Press
2301 Lucien Way #415
Maitland, FL 32751
407.339.4217
www.xulonpress.com

Printed in the United States of America
Paperback ISBN-13: 978-1-66283-899-6
Hard Cover ISBN-13: 978-1-66283-900-9
Ebook ISBN-13: 978-1-66283-901-6

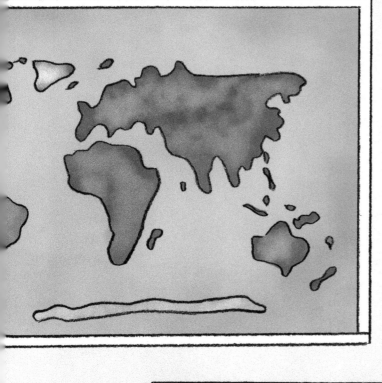

Spring time is
finally here, and
Junie can't wait
for Easter Break!

"Four days 13 hours and 27 minutes, until a basket filled with shiny grass, candy filled eggs, sugary marshmallows, and, fingers crossed, the water blaster 2000 squirt gun!" Junie said to the boy sitting next to her. "I can't wait for Easter!" "It's the next best thing to Christmas!" she exclaimed.

Junie stared at the clock. Then back to her teacher carrying on about some important battle in history. Growing more and more eager for the last day before break to end, Junie thought, "Just pass out the worksheet already so we can get on with it!"

Junie made it to the end of the day and
couldn't wait to get home.

She ran home from the bus stop burst into the door and said, "Any word? Any news from the Easter Bunny? Is he on his way? She ran into the living room, threw the couch pillows in the air…

looking for any signs. Something shiny, pink, yellow, blue, or green. "...Nothing yet..." she sighed. "Rats!"

"Junie, Easter is still a few days away," said her mother. "You have to wait for the Easter Bunny to come the night before. While you're sleeping."

And then she started to think…
who is the Easter Bunny anyway?
How does he know where I live?
Does he go to all the houses the
night before? How does he get my
Easter list? Is he watching me
to see if I have been bad
or good?

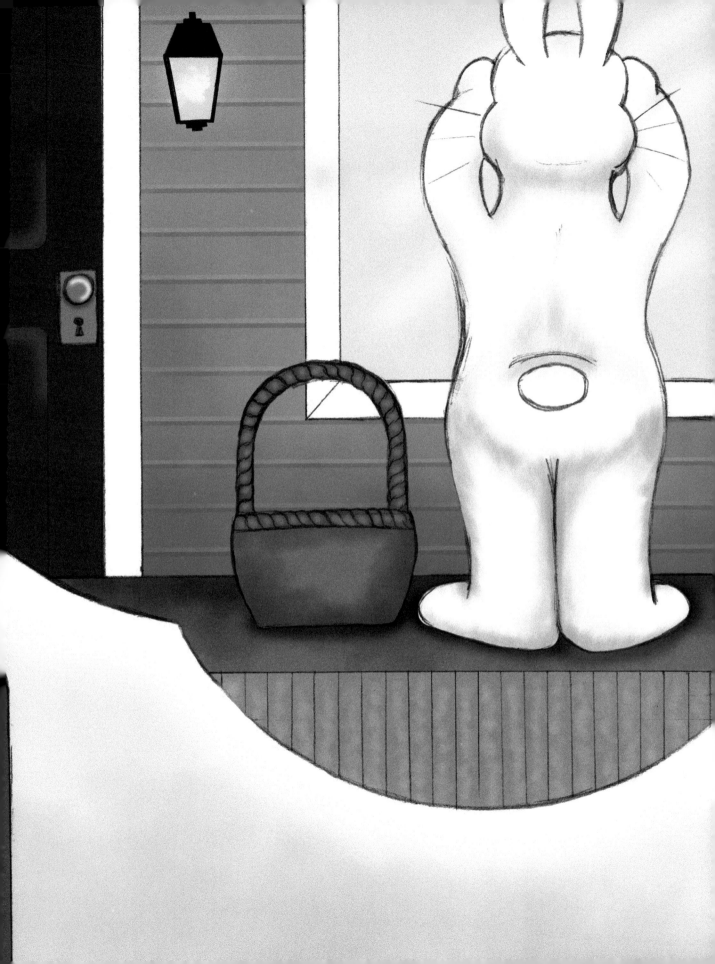

Junie sat at her desk in her room and began to brainstorm.
She made a list of all the Easter Bunny's characteristics:
> Big
> Happy
> Round Belly
> White
> Fluffy
> Likes me to leave him carrots
> Gives candy and toys
> Comes in the middle of the night

"You know", Junie thought, "He reminds me of someone…?" "Someone else very similar.

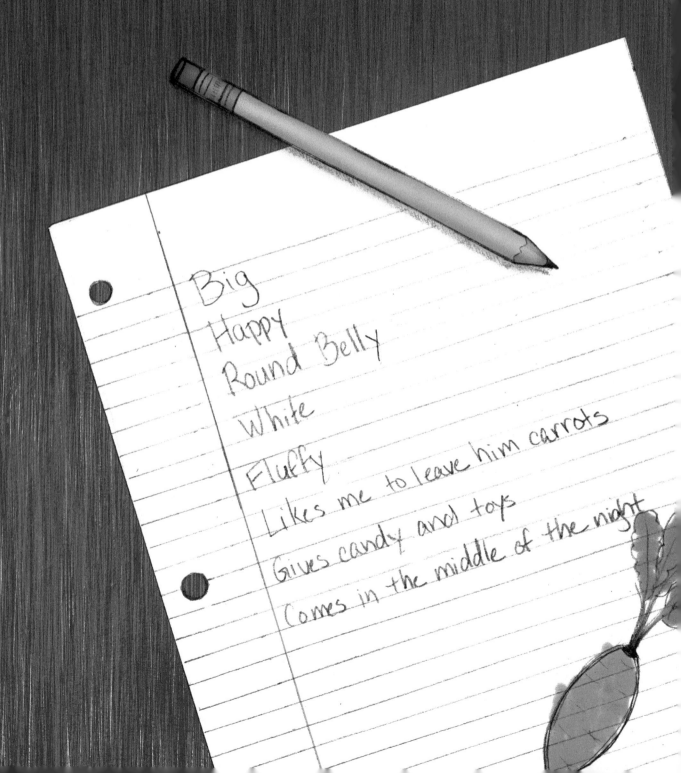

Big
Happy
Round Belly
White
Fluffy
Likes me to leave him carrots
Gives candy and toys
Comes in the middle of the night

Junie begins to make another list on the other side of her paper. I know someone else that is...

She thinks a minute staring at the two lists..." Seems so similar too..."

"Santa..!" Junie shouted. "That's it!" "The Easter Bunny must be Santa dressed up in a bunny costume!"

Big
Jolly
Round Belly
White Fluffy beard
Likes me to Leave him cookies
Gives candy and toys
Comes in the middle of the night.

She ran downstairs and began to explain her discovery, "Mom, it makes perfect sense. Santa already has all the kid's addresses, he already knows how to get to our house, he already has a workshop, and he already has a big belly."

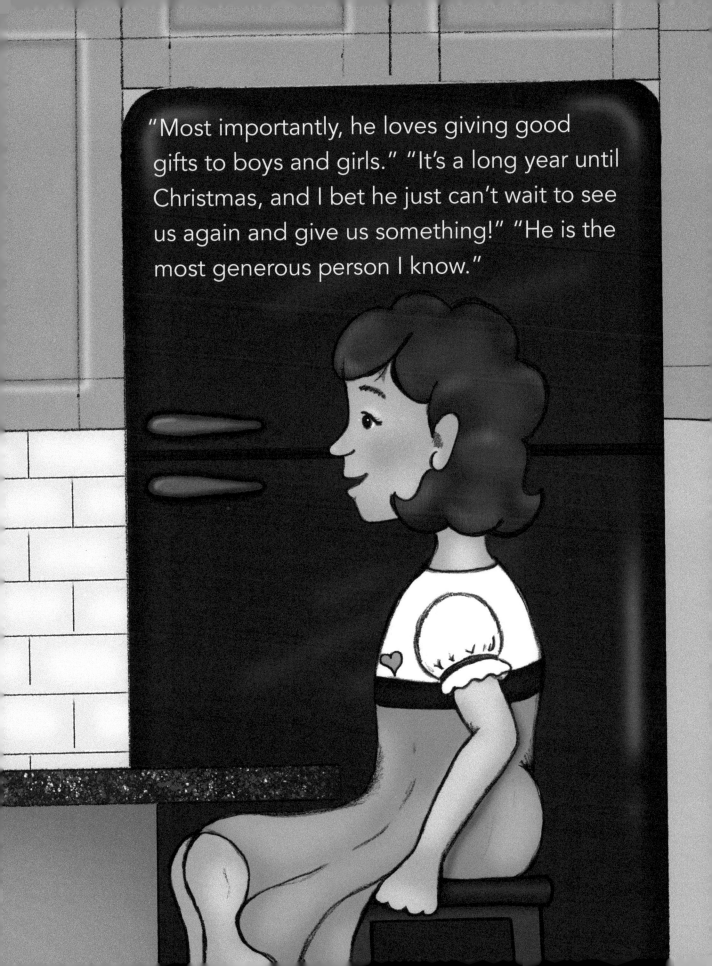

"Most importantly, he loves giving good gifts to boys and girls." "It's a long year until Christmas, and I bet he just can't wait to see us again and give us something!" "He is the most generous person I know."

She stopped to pause, "I wonder how he gets the eggs…?"

"The elves and reindeer paint them! Of course!"

"It all makes so much sense now!" said Junie. "And I bet in every season, no matter what, he is looking for ways to give good gifts to us!"

Her mom says, "Hmmm…now that reminds me of someone else I know." "Who could that be that is always looking for ways to bring us good gifts in every season?"

The mailman? Questioned Junie. "No, that's not it," said mom. "The ice cream truck?" "No…," added mom. The school bus driver?" "No, that's not it either." "Well… then…who is it?" Asked Junie.

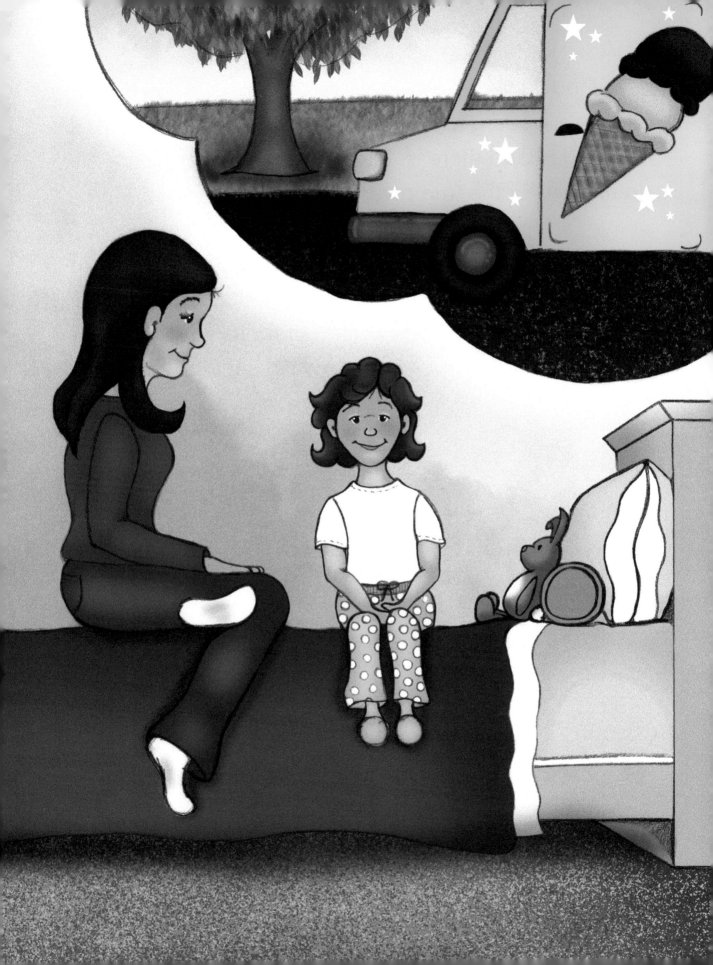

"It's God Junie." God is always looking for ways to bring us good gifts in every season, and he is the most generous God there is. Santa and the Easter Bunny all remind us of the true giver of good things, God.

That night as her mom tucked her in bed, she asked Junie, "Are you too excited to sleep? I know its been hard for you to wait for Easter." "I can wait mom", replied Junie. "I know the Easter bunny got my list because Santa never misses a letter, and God is always listening."

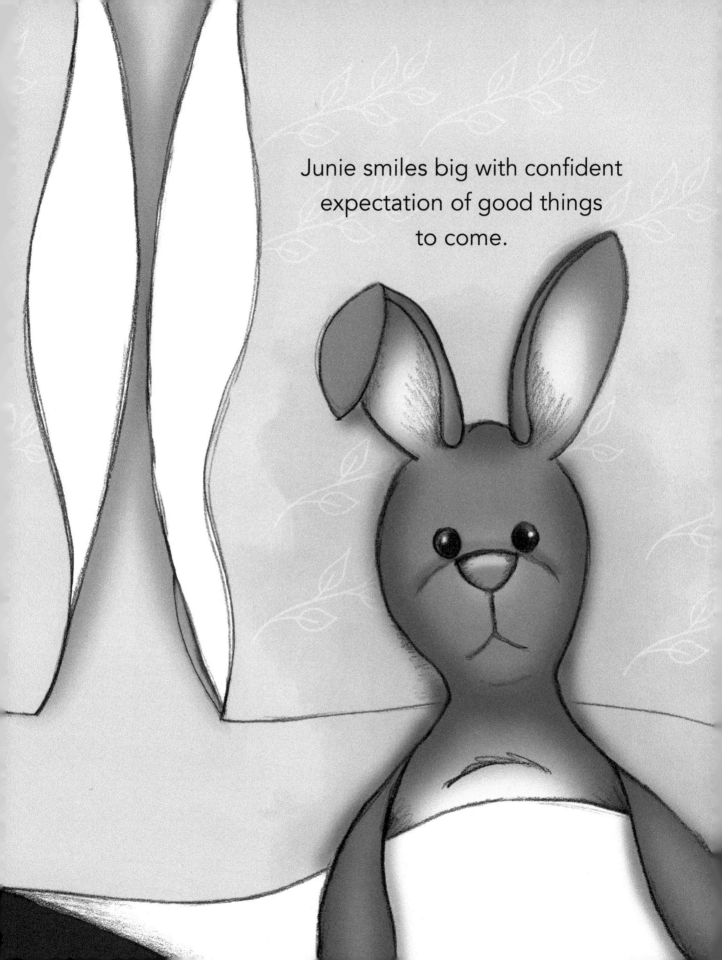

Junie smiles big with confident
expectation of good things
to come.

"Every good and perfect gift
is from above, coming down
from the Father of the heavenly
lights, who does not change
like shifting shadows."
James 1:17